The Nature Trail adventures of . . .

....

First published in Great Britain by HarperCollins *Children's Books* in 2021

1 3 5 7 9 10 8 6 4 2

ISBN: 978-0-00-845557-6

HarperCollins *Children's Books* is a division of HarperCollins*Publishers* Ltd
1 London Bridge Street, London SE1 9GF

www.harpercollins.co.uk

HarperCollins*Publishers*, 1st Floor, Watermarque Building, Ringsend Road, Dublin 4, Ireland

Printed in Poland

MIX
Paper from
responsible sources
FSC™ C007454

A PERCY THE PARK KEEPER BOOK

Percy the Park Keeper
Nature Trail
Activity Book

NICK BUTTERWORTH

HarperCollins *Children's Books*

Staying Safe

Be wise like Percy's friend the owl
and follow these nature-trail tips . . .

ALWAYS TAKE AN ADULT WITH YOU.

STAY ON THE PATH OR TRAIL.

DON'T TOUCH OR STROKE ANY ANIMALS.

KEEP AS QUIET AS POSSIBLE
TO AVOID DISTURBING WILDLIFE.
(AND THEN YOU'LL SEE MORE TOO!)

NEVER DISTURB AN ANIMAL'S HOME.

NEVER EAT ANYTHING YOU FIND ON THE TRAIL.

ALWAYS TAKE YOUR LITTER HOME WITH YOU.

"Thank you!"

Welcome to
Percy's Nature Trail!

Percy works hard looking after the park and his animal friends who live there. But Percy still likes to find time for some fun, so there is no one better to guide you as you discover the wildlife wonders of spring and summer!

Take this book on your walk and enjoy spotting nature outdoors. There are exciting ideas for indoor creative projects too, plus lots and lots of stickers. When you finish each page, don't forget to add your Percy or animal sticker!

"Have fun!"

Meet Percy's Friends!

Percy's animal friends are joining you on your
nature trail too. Get to know them here!

The **hedgehog** likes to
find a quiet place to sleep
– he's a bit shy!

The **squirrels** are great
explorers and know lots of secret
hiding places in Percy's park.

The friendly **fox** is always
trying to be helpful – but,
often, things don't go to plan!

The two **ducks** live on the lake. They
do everything together – usually with
plenty of splashing and quacking!

The clever **owl** spends a lot of time thinking.

Even Percy doesn't know how many **mice** there are – they never keep still enough to count!

The **rabbits** love playing games and having fun.

The **badger** comes to the rescue if anyone's in trouble and he's very brave.

The **mole** lives underground and sometimes comes up in unexpected places!

Percy's Packing List

Percy always likes to be prepared!

"Here are a few things you might need to take with you..."

Pencil	Raincoat
Notebook	Umbrella
Water	Sun cream
Snacks	Sunhat
Camera	Anti-bacterial hand gel
Binoculars	First-aid kit
Walking shoes or wellies	

"Let's go!"

Spring

Spring is one of Percy's favourite times of the year, when the days get longer and warmer after winter. New leaves begin to bud on the trees, bright blossoms appear and flowers start to poke through the soil. Bees and butterflies return, lots of baby animals are born and the birds are singing in Percy's park. What a happy time!

Take this book with you and join Percy on a spectacular spring nature trail!

Rainbow Colours

Add your Percy sticker!

The weather in spring can change quite quickly but Percy doesn't mind because, sometimes, when there is rain and sunshine at the same time, there will soon be a beautiful rainbow over his park!

"Finish the seven colours of the rainbow and then add your sun and cloud stickers."

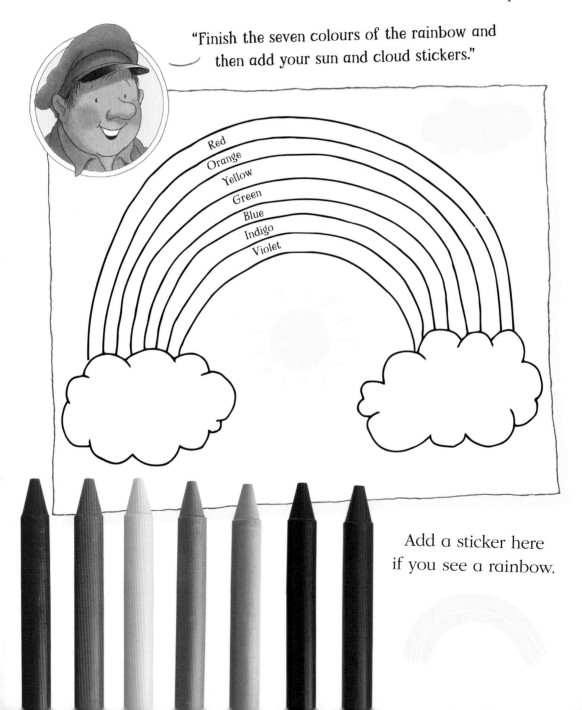

Red
Orange
Yellow
Green
Blue
Indigo
Violet

Add a sticker here if you see a rainbow.

Colour Treasure Hunt

Add your fox sticker!

Nature's colours are especially beautiful at this time of year when everything starts to spring back to life.

I found a red ....

I found an orange ....

I found a yellow ....

I found a green ....

I found a blue ....

I found an indigo ....

I found a violet ....

"Did you find something for every colour of the rainbow on your trail? Add a colour sticker for each one."

Lots of Leaves!

As the weather starts to get warmer, the squirrels in
Percy's park are delighted to see small green leaves
beginning to appear on the branches of the trees.
It's a sign that spring is truly on the way!

"Look out for different leaf shapes and draw
them here. How many kinds of leaves
can you see?"

Add your
squirrel
sticker!

Leaf Family

A fun activity for when you get home from your trail!

Add your mouse sticker!

"Find some leaves that you like and add stickers to give them funny faces. Here are some examples."

"Maybe you can find one that looks like Percy!"

"Or try turning one sideways, to look just like me!"

Blossoming Branches

Add your Percy sticker!

Percy's friend the owl loves spring too. When the branches of fruit trees are covered in pretty pink and white flowers, called blossoms, there is nowhere nicer to sit!

"Add your stickers to the branch to bring it alive with pink blossom for the owl!"

Can you spot these blossoms?
Add a white blossom sticker for each one you see.

Hawthorn blossom

Cherry blossom

Crab-apple blossom

Blooming Bulbs

The first flowers of spring grow from an underground bud called a "bulb", which stores food for the plant while it's resting in the soil.

"Please don't tell Percy, but I sometimes dig up his bulbs by mistake! Each of these flowers grows from a bulb. Add a daffodil sticker for each one that you spot."

Daffodil

Crocus

Bluebell

Snowdrop

Tulip

Hyacinth

Add your mole sticker!

Growing Wild!

There are so many wonderful wildflowers to see in the spring that Percy often thinks it's a shame to mow the grass in his park!

"How many of these wildflowers can you spot? Add a daisy sticker for each one."

Primrose

Daisy

Dandelion

Cornflower

Forget-me-not

Lesser celandine

Buttercup

Cow parsley

Violet

Cowslip

White clover

Red clover

What other wildflowers have you found?

....

....

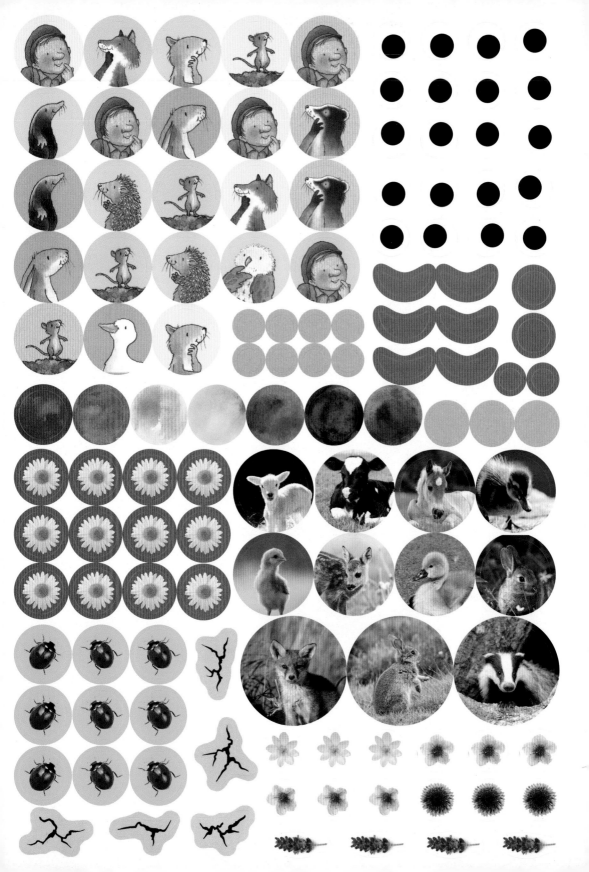

I
LOVE
SPRING!

Easter-egg Artist

Create some spectacular stripes!

YOU WILL NEED:
Tissue paper
Glue stick
An adult to help

"Tear up your tissue paper into little squares, and stick them on the egg to make colourful stripes. Then add your flower stickers to the stripes for a pretty finishing touch!"

"Happy Easter!"

Add your rabbit sticker!

Spring Babies

Add your Percy sticker!

Spring is the perfect time for baby birds and animals to be born because the weather is warmer and the days are longer.
What a busy season!

"Match your stickers to the baby animals to help them find their mothers."

Cow and calf
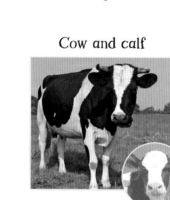

Horse and foal

Duck and duckling

Hen and chick

Deer and fawn

Sheep and lamb

Swan and cygnet

Rabbit and kitten

Burrow Babies

Some babies are born and raised underground,
until they are strong enough to go outside.

"Help each mother find the way to her baby,
then match a sticker to each one."

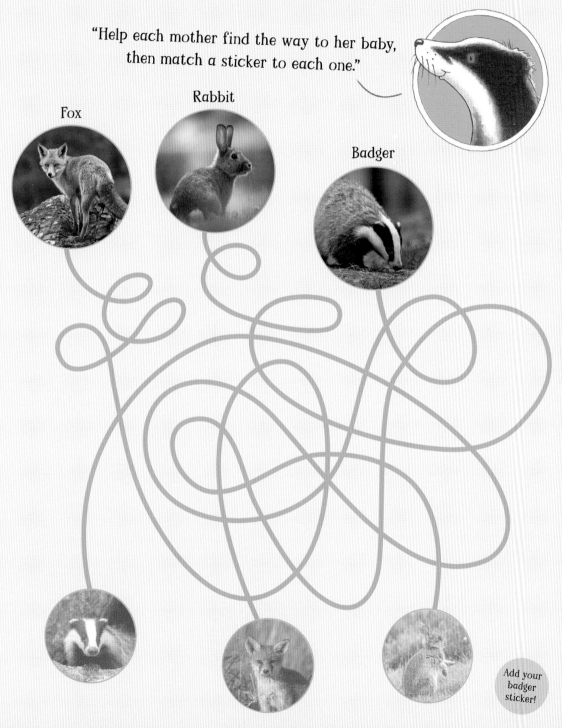

Fox

Rabbit

Badger

Add your
badger
sticker!

Clever Caterpillars

Add your mole sticker!

Caterpillars are incredible! After hatching from an egg, a caterpillar eats lots of leaves to grow big and strong enough to make a chrysalis. Then, after a few weeks, it emerges from its chrysalis as a beautiful butterfly!

Butterfly eggs
Look underneath leaves to find the tiny eggs.

Butterfly
What a beauty!

Caterpillar
Usually found munching on a leaf!

"Can you spot these four stages of a caterpillar's life? Add a leaf sticker for each one that you find."

Chrysalis
Try looking on the underside of a branch or twig.

Add some caterpillar stickers to munch on these leaves!

Flutter by, Butterfly!

Add your hedgehog sticker!

The first butterflies emerge in the spring.

"I wish I could fly!
Join the dashes to make a
butterfly appear. Then use
your crayons or pens to give it
brightly coloured wings."

Add your butterfly sticker when you are done.

Creepy Crawlies

Add your mouse sticker!

As it gets warmer and the first blossoms and flowers appear, lots of tiny insects and creepy crawlies wake up hungry from their winter sleep and go in search of food.

"How many of these little creatures can you spot? Add a ladybird sticker for each one."

Bee

Wasp

Ladybird

Caterpillar

Centipede

Earthworm

Spider

Beetle

Grasshopper

Pet Rock

Make your very own spring buddy!

YOU WILL NEED:
Tissue paper
Glue stick
An adult to help

"Find a smooth, flat rock or pebble while you are on your trail. Then paint it to make a cute pet who's very easy to look after!"

Add a ladybird sticker.

Add your fox sticker!

Busy Bees

In the spring bees come out to collect sticky nectar from flowers for food. As they work, a fine powder called "pollen" sticks to their furry bodies and is taken from one flower to the next, where it helps to make seeds so that new plants can grow.

"Draw and colour some more flowers and then add your bee stickers to each. Remember that bees love bright colours!"

Add your badger sticker!

Spring Sounds

Add your rabbit sticker!

Close your eyes and listen to the sounds of spring!

Bird singing

Insect buzzing

Lamb bleating

Cuckoo calling

Wind in the trees

Chick chirping

Rain falling

Woodpecker tapping

Calf mooing

"My long ears are perfect for hearing all the different springtime noises! How many did you hear? Add a bee sticker for each one."

What else can you hear?

....

Terrific Tadpoles!

Add your mouse sticker!

Frogs also lay eggs in the spring. Their eggs, or "spawn", turn into little tadpoles before eventually becoming frogs.

Frog spawn

Tadpole

"If you are by a stream or pond, look out for each of these stages of a frog's life cycle. Add a frog sticker for each one you spot."

Frog

Tadpole with legs

Froglet

Textures of Spring

Add your hedgehog sticker!

Stop on your trail and explore with your hands!

"Sometimes I wish I were soft, so Percy wouldn't have to wear gloves to pick me up! How many textures can you find? Add a feather sticker for each one."

Something soft ....

Something hard ....

Something smooth ....

Something fuzzy ....

Something rough ....

Something slimy ....

Something shiny ....

Something bumpy ....

Feathered Friends

There are so many different birds to see in the spring, and you will hear them singing to each other too!

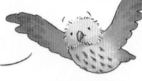

"Can you spot these birds on your trail? Add a bird sticker for each one."

Bluetit

Wren

Great tit

Chaffinch

Swift

Blackbird

Bullfinch

Woodpecker

Wood pigeon

What other birds can you see?

....

Add your owl sticker!

Nature Painting

Paint a springtime masterpiece!

"I'd love a new picture for the wall in my hut!
Find some feathers and twigs to take home, and then
use them as brushes to paint a picture of something
you found on your trail."

"Don't forget to sign your
name when you have
finished!"

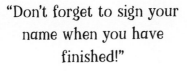

By ....

Date ....

Comfy Nests

Birds make nests in the spring, using dried grass, moss and feathers. Then they lay their eggs inside, which they sit on, keeping them nice and warm!

"Find some grass, short twigs and small stones on your trail. At home, arrange the grass and twigs in a small container to make your very own nest. Next add the stones as the eggs!"

Add a feather sticker if you see:

Nest

Eggshell

Feather

Add your mouse sticker!

Happy Hatchling!

When a baby bird is ready, it hatches out of its shell.
It's an exciting time for the ducks in Percy's park!

Add your duck sticker!

"This egg looks ready to hatch!
Add stickers to make some
cracks in the shell.

"Look — the egg has cracked open!
Draw a baby bird hatching out."

"Welcome to the
world, baby bird!
You look just like me
when I was a baby!"

Nature Trail Journal

"I hope you had fun on your spring trail!
Complete these sentences and add
a butterfly sticker for each one."

My favourite thing on the trail was ....

....

The most surprising thing on the trail was ....

....

The best place I visited was ....

....

The creature I liked best was ....

....

My favourite outdoor activity was ....

....

My favourite indoor activity was ....

....

The most interesting thing I learnt was ....

....

The best thing I found was ....

....

My favourite flower was ....

....

My favourite bird was ....

....

The biggest thing I found was ....

....

The smallest thing I found was ....

....

Nature Trail Notes

"Jot down your own notes here.
You can decorate them with your
extra springtime stickers!"

Spring Trail Certificate

This is to certify that

....

has completed Percy the Park Keeper's Spring Nature Trail.

Percy

The Park Keeper

Well done!
Give yourself
a sticker.

Summer

Summer is the hottest season of the year, when
the sun shines and the days are lighter for longer.
Trees are covered in green leaves, and some
grow fruit. Bees buzz around brightly
coloured flowers. No wonder Percy
loves the summer!

Take this book with you
and join Percy on a super
summer nature trail!

Beautiful Butterflies

Add your Percy sticker!

Percy looks forward to the summer, when beautiful butterflies bring colour to the park!

"How many of these butterflies can you spot? Add a butterfly sticker for each one."

Speckled wood

Holly blue

Red admiral

Meadow brown

Common blue

Peacock

Small white

Marbled white

Small tortoiseshell

What other butterflies have you seen?

....

Wonderful Wings

Design your own butterfly!

"Colour in the wings of this butterfly and then use your stickers to give it some beautiful spotty decorations!"

Then give yourself a butterfly sticker.

Marvellous Minibeasts!

A minibeast is a small animal that doesn't have a skeleton inside.
There are all sorts of them to find outside in the summertime
when the weather is warmer.

Grasshopper

Bee

Wasp

Ant

Caterpillar

Green beetle

"All of these creatures are even smaller than me!"

Black beetle

Ladybird

Butterfly

Fly

Centipede

Worm

Slug

Snail

Wood louse

"How many did you spot?
Give yourself a spider sticker
for each one."

Add your
mouse
sticker!

Tremendous Trees!

Add your owl sticker!

The trees in Percy's park look glorious in the summer when their branches are covered in bright green leaves.

"How many trees and their leaves can you spot? Add a matching leaf sticker for each one. Then choose a tree for me!"

Horse chestnut

Silver birch

Beech

Ash

Oak

Sycamore

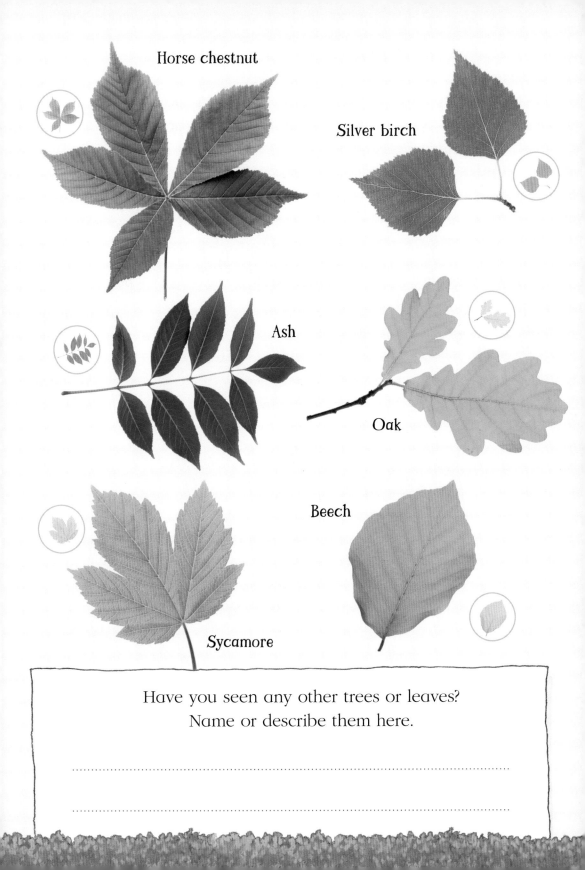

Horse chestnut

Silver birch

Ash

Oak

Beech

Sycamore

Have you seen any other trees or leaves?
Name or describe them here.

Bark Rubbing

Notice how different tree trunks have different
patterns and textures, rough and smooth.

"Why not have a go at bark rubbing? Hold some paper against
a tree trunk, then rub a crayon over the paper and watch the
pattern appear! Stick your best bark rubbing here."

Add your
Percy
sticker!

Hug a Tree!

Some people think that
hugging a tree can make
you feel lovely
and calm.

"Try hugging a tree when you are on your trail!
Shut your eyes and imagine what it's like to be me!
Write down here what it felt like to hug a tree."

....

....

....

All trees love a hug!

Add your
squirrel
sticker!

Wonderful Wildflowers

Add your rabbit sticker!

Percy's friends can often be found snoozing among the wildflowers on a hot summer day – what a wonderful place to be!

Daisy

Buttercup

Poppy

Cornflower

Cow parsley

Honeysuckle

Foxglove

Ragged robin

"How many wildflowers can you spot? Add a buttercup sticker for each one."

What other wildflowers have you seen?

....

....

Floral Fashion!

Make a daisy-chain crown,
belt or necklace to wear
on the trail!

"Pick daisies with long stems.
Cut a small slit halfway down the stem
of the first daisy using your thumbnail and
carefully thread through the stem of the next daisy.
Then make a slit in the stem of that daisy and keep
going with more daisies until you have a chain.
To close the chain, make a slit in the last daisy stem
a little longer than the others, and pull through
the head of the first daisy."

Add your
hedgehog
sticker!

Match your stickers to the
shapes to complete the
daisy chain.

Woodland Wonders

Add your fox sticker!

Go on a woodland scavenger hunt!

"Percy has given us a list of things to find. Can you help?
Add a cobweb sticker for each one you see."

Cobweb	Bark	Rock	Twig

 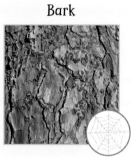  

Feather	Leaf	Tree stump	Fern

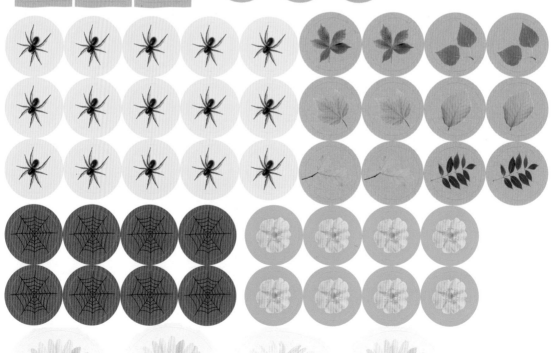

I
LOVE
SUMMER!

Twig Trail

Add your badger sticker!

The badger sometimes leaves arrows on the paths in Percy's park, so he doesn't get lost!

"Match your stickers to the shapes below to help me find my way back through the park! How about making your own twig trail for your friends to follow?"

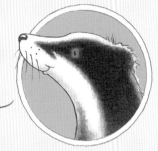

Animal-track Detective

Add your Percy sticker!

Animals can be hard to see in the wild, but they often leave behind clues with their paws.

"When we play hide-and-seek, I sometimes find my friends by following their tracks! Match your stickers to the shapes below to find out who was here."

Rabbit

Fox

Squirrel

Mouse

Badger

Mole

What other tracks have you found?

....

Handprint Fun!

Animals aren't the only ones to leave prints behind!

"Place your hand on this page. Then draw around it and colour it in to see what your prints look like!"

Add your hedgehog sticker!

Cloud Spotting

Add your Percy sticker!

On a summer day, Percy and his friends like nothing more than relaxing on the grass, watching the clouds float past in the blue sky!

Cumulus

Cirrus

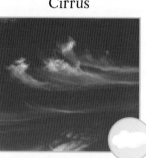

Stratus

Cumulonimbus

Stratocumulus

Altocumulus

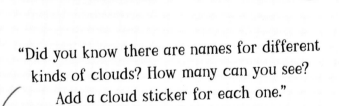

"Did you know there are names for different kinds of clouds? How many can you see? Add a cloud sticker for each one."

Cloud Shapes

Sometimes clouds can look like objects or animals.

"What shapes have you seen in the clouds?
Draw some of them here.

Add your
mouse
sticker!

Make a Sundial

Add your mole sticker!

One of the best things about the summer is, of course, the sunshine, which you can even use to tell the time!

"On your trail collect one long twig and twelve small stones to take home. Stick the long twig in the ground and at 12 o'clock, midday, place one stone where the twig's shadow falls.

"Add your number twelve sticker to the stone. At 1 o'clock, place another stone where the twig's shadow falls and add your number one sticker, and so on, until 6 o'clock in the afternoon. Then carry on in the morning at 7 o'clock, until you have used all your stones."

Give yourself a sun sticker!

Spectacular Sunset!

Add your Percy sticker!

When Percy leads the animals home each evening, they always take time to stop and admire the beautiful sunset. It's the most magical time of day!

"Ask an adult to watch the sunset with you and then use your crayons to fill this page with all the amazing colours in the sky. Add a sticker for each colour you see. And a sunset sticker!"

Seaside Sightings

Add your duck sticker!

The two ducks often wonder what it would be like to live by the sea, instead of the lake in Percy's park!

"If you are lucky enough to go to the beach, see how many of these things you can find. Add a seashell sticker for each one!"

Seagull

Seashell

Seaweed

Waves

Driftwood

Fossil

Crab

Pebbles

Rock pool

Rock Pool Scavenger Hunt

There are lots of interesting things
to find in rock pools too!

"Add a starfish sticker for each one you find."

Something soft ....

Something hard ....

Something smooth ....

Something bumpy ....

Something round ....

Something wiggly ....

Something slimy ....

Something pointy ....

Add your
rabbit
sticker!

Summer Sounds

On your trail, close your eyes and listen
to the wonderful sounds of summer!

"There's so much going on outside in the summer!
How many noises can you hear? Add a
bird sticker for each one."

Bird singing

Bee buzzing

Frog croaking

Seagull squawking

Fly buzzing

Grasshopper chirping

River flowing

Duck quacking
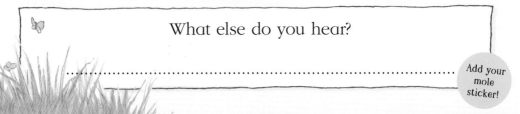

Waves lapping

What else do you hear?

....

Add your
mole
sticker!

Summer Exhibition

Add your badger sticker!

Put on a show of your summer nature-trail finds!

"I love collecting things I find, like feathers, leaves and pebbles! How about displaying your outdoor treasures for your friends and family to admire? Isn't nature amazing! Draw your favourite things in the frames above."

Nature Trail Journal

"Did you enjoy your summer nature trail?
Complete these sentences and add
a seashell sticker for each one."

My favourite thing on the trail was ....

....

The most surprising thing on the trail was ....

....

The best place I visited was ....

....

The creature I liked best was ....

....

My favourite outdoor activity was ....

....

My favourite indoor activity was ....

....

The most interesting thing I learnt was ....

....

The best thing I found was ....

....

My favourite flower was ....

....

My favourite bird was ....

....

The biggest thing I found was ....

....

The smallest thing I found was ....

....

Add your squirrel sticker!

Nature Trail Notes

"Jot down your own notes here.
You can decorate them with
your extra summer stickers!"

Summer Trail Certificate

This is to certify that

....

has completed Percy the Park Keeper's Summer Nature Trail.

Percy

The Park Keeper

Well done!
Give yourself
a sticker.